The Girl, The Bear and the Magic Shoes

For Josephine ~ JD

For András and Ádám ~ LM

First published 2018 by Macmillan Children's Books
an imprint of Pan Macmillan
20 New Wharf Road, London N1 9RR
Associated companies throughout the world
www.panmacmillan.com

ISBN: 978-1-4472-7597-8

1 3 5 7 9 8 6 4 2

A CIP catalogue record for this book is available
from the British Library.

Printed in China.

WRITTEN BY
JULIA DONALDSON

ILLUSTRATED BY
LYDIA MONKS

MACMILLAN CHILDREN'S BOOKS

There once was a little girl called Josephine who loved running. Her old running shoes were too tight, so she went into a shoe shop and tried on some new ones. They were red and they had a label saying 'Magic Shoes'.

“What’s magic about them?” asked Josephine.
“Aha! Wait and see,” said the shoe-shop lady.
Josephine bought the shoes and decided to go for a run.

Pit-a-pat, pit-a-pat, went the shoes.
But then she heard another sound: Click-click! Click-click!
Josephine turned round.
A bear with a backpack was following her!

Click-click! went his claws on the road.
Josephine ran faster. So did the bear.
Pit-a-pat, click-click!

The road went uphill. Up and up it went, until it stopped at the bottom of a snowy mountain. Josephine stopped too.

"I'll never get up that," she said.

"Yes you will,
Oh yes you will.
Just start climbing
And don't stand still," came a voice – or rather, two voices.

The voices seemed to be coming from Josephine's feet. Josephine looked down and was amazed to see her new running shoes change into . . .

. . . blue snow boots.

Crunch, crunch, crunch!
Josephine crunched her way up the snowy mountain.
But – Crunch, crunch, crunch! – the bear was still behind her.

Josephine reached the top of the mountain.
The other side was very steep.
"I'll never get down there," she said.

"Yes you will,
Oh yes you will.
Just start skiing
And don't stand still," came the two voices.

Josephine looked down and saw that she
was wearing a pair of green skis.

Whee! Whizz! Josephine skied down the mountain.
But – Whee! Whizz! Behind her, the bear was sliding
down on his bottom.

At the foot of the mountain was a bog. The mud was thick and deep.
"I'll never get through this," said Josephine.

“Yes you will,
Oh yes you will.
Just start squelching
And don’t stand still,” came the two voices, and the skis turned into . . .

. . . yellow wellies!

Squelch, squelch, squelch!
Josephine squelched through the bog.
But – Squelch, squelch, squelch! – the bear
was still coming after her.

Josephine came to a lake. "I'll never get across," she said.

“Yes you will,
Oh yes you will.
Just start swimming
And don’t stand still,” came the voices again, and the wellies turned into . . .

. . . orange flippers!

Splish, splash! Josephine swam across the lake.
But – Splish, splash! – the bear was swimming after her.
He was getting closer!

"I'm getting too tired to swim," thought Josephine.
But then she came to an island in the middle of the lake.

Josephine waded out of the water.
She kicked off her flippers and climbed up a tree.

The bear climbed out and stood at the bottom of the tree.
"Come down!" he called.

"But you'll eat me," said Josephine.
"No I won't," said the bear.
"Then why were you chasing me?" asked Josephine.

“I was chasing you because you left your old shoes behind in the shop,” said the bear. “The shoe-shop lady asked me to give them back to you,” and he took them out of his backpack.

Josephine climbed down the tree.
"Thank you," she said. "But what were you doing in the shop? Bears don't need shoes, do they?"
"Oh, that was a mistake," said the bear. "I didn't mean to go into the shoe shop. I meant to go into the fish shop next door."

Then the flippers laughed:
"Ha ha ha!
Ho ho ho!
Time for a dance now –
Off you go!"
and they turned into a pair of pink dancing shoes.

Josephine put the dancing shoes on, and she
and the bear danced all around the island . . .

. . . until it was time to splash,

squelch,

crunch,

whizz

and run

all the way home.